S   the
lunc   ing
a pi   g it
craz   nd
dow   ts!
Atte
"   ck.
"Is—
"   on-
de   he
pie
"   lis
El   e!"

Look for these other LUNCHROOM titles:

LUNCHROOM

SPACE FOOD

Ann Hodgman

Illustrated by Roger Leyonmark

SPLASH™

B

A BERKLEY / SPLASH BOOK

LUNCHROOM #8, SPACE FOOD, is an original publication of The Berkley Publishing Group. This work has never appeared before in book form.

A Berkley Book/published by arrangement with General Licensing Company, Inc.

PRINTING HISTORY
Berkley edition/December 1990

ISBN: 0-425-12441-X
RL: 4.8

A BERKLEY BOOK® TM 757,375
Berkley Books are published by The Berkley Publishing Group, 200 Madison Avenue, New York, New York 10016.
The name "BERKLEY" and the "B" logo are trademarks belonging to Berkley Publishing Corporation.

PRINTED IN THE UNITED STATES OF AMERICA

10 9 8 7 6 5 4 3 2 1

Chapter One

Space and Spies

"Mommy, I'm wheezing!" complained the little girl on the television screen.

"I know, honey," her television mother answered tenderly. "And I've got just the thing for that cough of yours."

The little girl squinched up her face in make-believe worry. "But I hate nasty medicines!" she whined.

"This isn't nasty!" her television mother assured her. "This is Choco-Bronch, the first *cough* syrup that tastes like *chocolate* syrup! Rich, soothing chocolate flavor loaded with—"

"Diego, turn that thing off!"

Ten-year-old Diego Lopez turned around to see his father standing in the kitchen doorway. "Oh, good morning, Dad," he said.

"It will be a *better* morning when the mind rotter is turned off," his father told him. "You know the rule, Diego! Now go get dressed."

The rule in the Lopez house was that you could only watch television if you could prove that it was educational. And you had to prove it in advance. Diego's parents were both teachers, and they didn't approve of the mind rotter—as Mr. Lopez liked to call the TV *every single time*.

"I'm not really watching it, Dad," Diego protested. "I'm just waiting for the news to come back on. I think they're going to be showing—Wait, here it comes!"

The perky sound of a synthesized flute filled the air. "Welcome to A.M. *Pasadena*, with your host, Mike McIntyre," said an announcer. Now Mike McIntyre's smooth pink face filled the screen. "Good morning, everyone," he said with a big grin. "Top stories in the news this morning are—"

"Hey, no fair! How come he gets to watch TV?"

Diego's little brother Carlos had just come into the kitchen. He was walking toward the cereal cupboard backward, so that he could stare accusingly at his father and the TV screen at the same time.

"...Elephants don't like cats, you say?" continued Mike McIntyre on TV. "Try telling that

2

to the kitten that little Timmy Nolan found in the—"

"Diego, this isn't news!" said Mr. Lopez. "This is just mind-rotting fluff! Now would you please—"

"Anyway, it's not fair that *he* gets to—" began Carlos again.

"Wait! Quiet, both of you! Here it is!" Diego interrupted. A close-up of NASA's newest space station filled the screen.

"...the *Orion,* which goes into orbit in just under four weeks," came Mike McIntyre's voice. "As most of you know, the *Orion* will become the nation's first manned space station to remain in orbit for an entire month. Thirty astronauts will be aboard—the largest crew in NASA's history."

Both Carlos and Mr. Lopez sat silently down at the kitchen table to watch.

"Because the crew will be spending such a long time in orbit, special efforts are being made to keep them comfortable," said Mike McIntyre. "Their living quarters are the most homelike in NASA's history. They will have satellite television and—"

"A mind rotter in *space?*" interrupted Mr. Lopez. "Is that what you call progress?"

"Dad, *shhh!*" hissed Diego and Carlos at the same time.

3

"—NASA is working to provide more interesting food than was available on earlier voyages," continued the anchorman. "Whether all these efforts will keep the astronauts from feeling homesick remains to be seen.

"We'll keep you informed on the *Orion*'s voyage as the weeks progress toward takeoff date," promised Mike McIntyre. "And now here's Holly Bergman with the weather update for all you water-skiers out there...."

Diego leaned back in his chair and sighed. "I wish I could go with them," he said as the space station's picture was replaced by a weather map.

"Hey, maybe you can, D!" said Carlos excitedly. He always called Diego "D." "You could call NASA and tell them what a genius you are! I bet the astronauts would *like* to have you come with them! You would remind them of their own kids, except smarter!"

"I think it's probably too late now," Diego told him. "They've already picked the people who get to go up in orbit and do a lot of experiments and become famous." He sighed again. "While *I* get to go to sixth grade, as usual."

"You won't even get to do that if you don't hurry up," said his father. "Look at the clock! It's almost—"

"It's almost time for the bus to get here!" came the outraged voice of Diego's mother at the back door. She had just been out for a run.

"Look at you!" she panted, mopping her forehead with the sleeve of her sweatshirt. "All *three* of you watching television! What on earth got into you? You know the rules!"

Diego got to the bus stop just in time to see the bus pulling away. Since one of his own private rules was that you should never embarrass yourself by running after a bus, he was late to school. He arrived as the Pledge of Allegiance was starting on the public-address system.

Since *another* of Diego's private rules was that it was okay to skip the Pledge of Allegiance, he slowed from a trot to a walk as he headed toward his sixth-grade classroom. And when he slowed down, he noticed the stranger.

The stranger was a tall, skinny blond man in a too-big gray suit. He was tiptoeing down the hall, peeking into each classroom he passed. Every few seconds he darted a quick look over his shoulder, as though he was afraid of being noticed.

New teacher, maybe, Diego thought. *He doesn't want anyone to know he's lost.* "Can I help you find something?" Diego asked him.

"Oh!" The man whirled around to face Diego. "I . . . I . . . no, thank you!" he stammered. "I'm not lost. I'm, uh, just taking a walk." He gave Diego a flustered smile. "Nice morning for a walk, isn't it?"

"Sure," Diego said after a second. It was a nice morning *outside*, anyway. Diego could hear the pledge winding down on the P.A. system. "Have a nice day," he said, and ducked into his homeroom.

"Sorry I'm late, Mrs. Doubleday," Diego told his teacher as he scurried to his seat. "I missed the bus."

Mrs. Doubleday never got upset about little things. "That's okay, Diego," she said. "I'm glad you're here. Could you take out your English books, gang? Today we're starting our section on punctuation."

Everyone groaned.

"We *know* how to punctuate things, Mrs. Doubleday," said Junior Smith. "It's a waste of the taxpayers' dollars teaching us stuff we already know!"

Junior's main interest in life was money—how to make it and how to save it. Lately he had embarked on a big campaign to protect taxpayers. "After all, I'm going to *be* a taxpayer in a couple of years!" he liked to explain.

6

Mrs. Doubleday smiled at him. "Actually, Junior, you could use a little work on commas. I didn't see a single one in that last report you wrote."

"Oh, I know when to use them. I just didn't want to waste ink," Junior told her. "Ink is money, you know."

"As far as you're concerned, *everything* is money," Bonnie Kirk muttered.

"Anyway, commas are cute!" said Jennifer Stevens. (*Her* main interest—besides herself—was how things looked.) "They really set off words nicely. I use them all the time."

"You certainly do," said Mrs. Doubleday, "even when it's incorrect to do so. So this section will probably be good for you, too. Could you all please turn to page—"

"Who's that man?"

Tiffany Root, her eyes wide with fear, was pointing at the door.

Everyone turned, but there was no one there.

"A m-m-man was looking in at us!" stammered Tiffany. "A really c-c-creepy man!"

"Way to go, Tiff!" chortled Jonathan Matterhorn. "Now you're scared of things that aren't even there!"

If worrying could be called a main interest, it was Tiffany's. She was the most nervous person Diego had ever seen. This time, though, Diego was sure Tiffany wasn't imagining things.

"Was it a blond guy?" he asked her, and Tiffany nodded. "I saw him, too," Diego told Mrs. Doubleday. "He was kind of hanging around the hall."

"Lying in wait for one of us, maybe!" said Tiffany with a frightened gasp. "I bet he's an escaped criminal or something!"

"Okay, guys, let's cut the chatter," said Mrs. Doubleday briskly. "I didn't see this man, Tiffany, but I'm sure that whoever he is, he's not lying in wait for any of us. He's probably just lost."

"But he told me he *wasn't* lost!" protested Diego.

"All right, so he's not lost. But whoever he is, he's not *half* as important to our class as commas are."

"Does anyone know what's for lunch today?" asked Rocky Latizano.

Once nine o'clock in the morning rolled around, Rocky's thoughts began to drift toward lunch. By eleven in the morning, he started sighing impatiently and tapping his watch. And now that the sixth-graders were actually on their way to the lunchroom, there was no point in talking to Rocky about anything *but* lunch.

"I hope it isn't one of Ms. Weinstock's barfo health casseroles," he said loudly.

A month ago Ms. Weinstock, Hollis Elementary School's dietician, had gone away for a few weeks work with a software company on a program for the lunchroom's new central-processing computer. Unfortunately, being away seemed to have given her lots of inspiration—bad inspiration. Ever since she had been back, she had been trying out truly weird lunch combinations. There was nothing like black bean spaghetti and tofu meatballs with sprout sauce to make you appreciate a good old tuna melt.

"If she makes us eat any more of that asparagus loaf I'm going to—" Then Rocky broke off and pointed down the hall. "Hey! Is that the guy Tiffany was talking about?"

It certainly was. He was hunched up at the edge of the lunchroom door, peering furtively inside.

"The lunchroom is for students only," Rocky bellowed. "What do you want?"

The man jerked his head up, startled. "Oh, nothing!" he said hastily. He began to stroll casually away down the hall.

He might have looked more innocent if he hadn't kept peeking over his shoulder to see if they were watching him.

"We've got to call the police!" Tiffany said.

"After lunch, Tiff," Rocky told her calmly.

They were just walking through the lunchroom door themselves now. When they got inside, Rocky let out a groan. "Oh, no," he said. "Ms. Weinstock's sitting at the computer. That means she's planning a lot of horrible *new* lunches."

Ms. Weinstock was bent over the lunchroom computer. Her fingers were flying rapidly over the keyboard. "Hi, everyone," she greeted them as they came in. "This new computer is so fantastic! I've got lunches planned for the next eight years!"

In all of Pasadena—in all of the country, probably—only Hollis Elementary School had a lunchroom computer that would let Ms. Weinstock do something like that. But *everything* in Hollis Elementary School's lunchroom was fantastic, from the neon signs decorating the walls to the milkshake maker that could serve thirty people at once to the automated peanut-butter spreader.

"I'm glad the program's finally working okay," said Diego. He was always interested in anything to do with computers. "What are we having today?"

Ms. Weinstock looked a little embarrassed. "Well, I accidentally erased my menu for today. So we're having tuna fish sandwiches and potato chips."

Rocky beamed. "I'm first in line!" he shouted, and galloped toward the kitchen.

A few minutes later, Diego, Rocky, and a few other kids from Mrs. Doubleday's class were sitting down at one of the lunchroom tables. "I hope that creepy guy doesn't come back," Tiffany fretted. "I mean, I hope he *will* come back, so we can arrest him. I think he looks very suspicious. I think he's up to something. Do you think we should call the police or make a citizen's arrest?"

Chantilly Lace put down her sandwich and stared at Tiffany for a moment. "Tiffany, you can't arrest someone just because he *looks* suspicious! Besides, do you really think that he would be so . . . so out in the open if he were a crook or something," she demanded.

Before Tiffany could answer, Mr. Haypence burst through the lunchroom door like a rocket.

He was holding a piece of paper in his hand and flapping it crazily in the air. He was also jumping up and down and hollering, "Attention

11

all students! Attention, all students!"

"Mr. Haypence!" gasped Ms. Weinstock. "Is
... is anything the matter?"

"Nothing's the matter! Everything is wonderful!" cried Mr. Haypence. He shoved the
piece of paper toward her.

"Read this! Read this!" he shouted.

*"Hollis Elementary School is going into outer
space!"*

Chapter Two

Assignment: Space Food

"Going into space? What do you mean?" asked Diego blankly.

"The *Orion* space station! We're going on the *Orion*!" Mr. Haypence was practically screaming now. He looked as though he were about to blast off himself.

There was a stunned silence in the lunchroom. Then everyone began talking at once.

"But I can't go into space! I get airsick!" Tiffany wailed.

"Do you mean we're all going to be *astronauts*?" called Bob Kelly.

"Will we get paid?" asked Junior Smith. "How much do astronauts make, anyway?"

"Mr. Haypence, is this really going to happen?"

That was Diego. And when Mr. Haypence

heard him, he stopped flapping his piece of paper around.

"Well, *we're* not exactly going into space," he admitted. Then, as he saw the disappointed faces staring at him, he hurried to say, "But it's almost as good, I promise you!"

Mr. Haypence leaped onto the stage at the far end of the lunchroom. He flipped a switch on the podium and tapped experimentally on the microphone. Everyone held their hands over their ears as a cracking sound louder than the boomingest thunder shook the room. Mr. Haypence looked embarrassed and fiddled with the switches some more.

"Sorry about that," he said into the microphone. "May I have everyone's attention, please?" The room quieted down. "I have an important announcement to make: Hollis Elementary School has been chosen to create the first fun food for astronauts to take aboard the *Orion* space station."

"How did we get picked?" Bonnie wondered out loud.

"Who picked us?" asked Bob.

"Why us?" moaned Tiffany.

"Will we get paid for this?" Junior wanted to know.

Mr. Haypence held up his hand. "Please calm

down," he said. "I'll be happy to answer your questions one...at...a...time. Bonnie Kirk?"

"I don't understand, Mr. Haypence," she said. "Were we entered in some kind of contest or something?"

"Well, not exactly, Bonnie," Mr. Haypence told her. "You see, it was really a combination of things. First, I read in a school journal that NASA was considering asking school-children to come up with ideas for new astronaut food. It seems that the biggest problem with the stuff they have now is that it's not very interesting. It's healthy as all get-out, but not very flavorful. So NASA wondered if some of the nation's schools couldn't come up with better ideas for the space laboratories to experiment with. But the space agency just didn't have enough money to fund a nationwide school survey, let alone cull through the results to find an idea worth experimenting with.

"At about the same time, I got a call from Harlan Frantz. He was once a Hollis student himself, and now he's a very important man in the space-technology business. He works very closely with NASA on a number of projects, and has become quite wealthy as a result of his expertise. He's also been keeping up with his old school, and was very impressed with some of the things he's heard about lately. Things such as our very successful science fair and our Kidz in Charge restaurant program. Not to mention our fabulous, state-of-the-art computerized lunchroom.

"So one thing led to another and Mr. Frantz decided to pay for a program here at Hollis where the sixth-grade students will try to develop a new space food." Mr Haypence looked around the room with a thousand-watt smile on his face. "People, you're going to be inventing your own *space food!*"

This time, Mr. Haypence had no reason to be disappointed with his audience's reaction. Everyone in the lunchroom burst into cheers.

This is too good to be true! thought Diego. *Mr. Haypence must have gotten mixed up somehow!*

He raised his hand. "Is this okay with NASA?" he asked Mr. Haypence incredulously above the noise.

"It certainly is! NASA has announced that it *welcomes* Mr. Frantz's contribution!" shouted Mr. Haypence. "He will fund the entire project himself, and you can use the lunchroom as your laboratory!"

"Oh, no," said Ms. Weinstock.

Mr. Haypence didn't hear that, either. He was too busy scrutinizing the lunchroom. "Let's see," he mused. "We're going to turn the entire lunchroom over to the sixth grade for the next few weeks. The rest of the classes can eat lunch in their classrooms. We'll rip out the microwave oven and install some Bunsen burners instead. We'll need to set up experiment stations for each student, of course, and ... and ..."

Mr. Haypence didn't even notice the look of horror on Ms. Weinstock's face. He turned to Diego. "Diego, what else would we need to turn this lunchroom into a proper lab?" Everyone knew Diego had his own laboratory at home. When it came to science, he was the smartest kid at Hollis.

"Well, we don't need to make changes right away," he told the principal, trying to hide a grin. "Why don't we come up with a few ideas first, then see what kind of equipment we need."

"My feelings exactly!" said Mr. Haypence quickly. Ms. Weinstock gave a big sigh of relief.

"Can we start working on our recipes right away?" Rocky Latizano wanted to know. "Because I've got some fantastic dessert ideas, only I need to sample a lot of regular desserts first to make sure I'm on the right track!"

"If we come up with a good idea, do we get to copyright it?" Junior called out.

"Do you think we'll become famous?" Jenni-

17

fer Stevens wondered. "I mean, will we get to be on national television?"

"Don't we need to wear special lab coats and gas masks if we're going to be doing experiments?" Tiffany worried. "Where will we get everything we need?"

Mr. Haypence held up his hand for silence. "You'll get the answers to *all* your questions tomorrow," he said. "Because we're taking a field trip to the laboratory where Mr. Frantz works. He'll fill you in on what he's looking for, and he'll share his thoughts on how you can best provide it. He is a great thinker, a man of our time.

"After all," Mr. Haypence added, "when the eyes of the nation are upon you, you really need the advice of a great thinker."

And not just someone like you, Mr. Haypence, Diego said to himself.

The small auditorium at Lampert Laboratories, where Harlan Frantz worked, was a very comfortable place. The velvet seats were deep and cushiony, the carpet was thick and spongy, and the lights overhead cast a gentle, rosy light over the highly polished chrome and glass decorations.

The sixth-graders at Hollis had noticed all of

these details because they had been sitting in those velvet seats for almost half an hour now. Mr. Frantz was running a little late. The kids were getting a little restless.

"He's probably busy thinking about something," Diego remarked sourly to Bob Kelly, who was sitting next to him way in the back.

"Probably," Bob agreed. "You know these great thinkers. Speaking of thinking...have you done any thinking about what kind of space food you're going to work on?"

"Well, it's got to be supernutritious, of course," said Diego. "And it shouldn't take up too much space, so it can pack easily. And it should have enough calories so that they'll only need to eat once a day."

Bob looked impressed. "That sounds awesome. Can you really make—wait a minute! Is that Mr. Frantz?"

A small, portly man was walking onto the stage. He had a long fringe of black hair and was wearing a dark blue suit made out of some kind of hairy material.

"Harlan!" Mr. Haypence called from the front row. "It's wonderful to see you again!"

Mr. Frantz didn't answer.

"Oooooh," Tiffany whispered in awe. "He looks so *smart!*"

He was, indeed, staring thoughtfully out at his audience—staring and not saying anything. Gradually the auditorium grew quiet. Then, as Mr. Frantz continued to stare silently and thoughtfully at the audience, everyone started talking again.

Suddenly Mr. Frantz held out his hand. Once again, everyone fell silent.

"Fun," said Mr. Frantz solemnly.

"I beg your pardon, Harlan?" Mr. Haypence said questioningly.

"Fun," repeated Mr. Frantz. "The space food must be *fun*. That is my only requirement."

His mouth snapped shut.

Mr. Haypence was looking worried now. "When you say fun, do you mean fun to eat or fun to make?" he asked.

"Fun," said Mr. Frantz simply. "I will pay whatever it costs to develop the food and ship it to NASA. I will allow the sixth-graders total freedom to develop whatever they want."

Now Mrs. Doubleday and a few of the other teachers began to look a little bewildered, too.

"All I ask is that the food you invent be *fun*," said Mr. Frantz. "Today is Thursday. The space station leaves in three and a half weeks. Three weeks from next Monday, I will charter a plane and have your space food flown to NASA. As long as it is fun."

He bowed, pivoted on his heel, and walked off the stage.

For a moment no one knew quite what to do. Then Mr. Haypence got slowly to his feet.

"There speaks a great thinker, don't you agree?" he asked in an awed voice. "Such a great thinker that he knows he can leave all the planning up to *us!*"

Diego didn't agree at all. *That guy's no thinker,* he said to himself. *He doesn't even care if the food is good for the astronauts or not! Well, I'm not going to pay any attention to this "fun" thing. I'm sure I can—*

Suddenly Diego realized that Mrs. Doubleday was talking. "As long as we've come all the way out to these labs, shouldn't we do our planning here?" she asked Mr. Haypence. "The seats are comfortable, anyway."

"We don't have *time* to plan!" wailed Tiffany. "If we've only got three and a half weeks, shouldn't we go right back to the lunchroom and start cooking? Or inventing? Or whatever it is we're going to be doing?"

"Certainly," agreed Mr. Haypence. "The instant we're back at school, you may all begin work. We'll need to turn the entire time between now and the launch over to space food. Teachers, will you be able to help with that?"

Mrs. Doubleday nodded enthusiastically. "This is a very important project," she said. "I don't see why our classes can't be tied in with the work the kids will be doing in the lunchroom! Take English, for instance. We can read cookbooks and learn how to write recipes!"

"Oh, goody!" Diego whispered to Bob.

"And in math, we can learn about the measurements the kids will need when they're coming up with their formulas," chimed in Mr. Levin, another sixth-grade teacher. "Maybe we'll finally learn the metric system, too!" (Mr. Levin was always trying to get kids to use the metric system.)

"I can hardly wait," Bob whispered to Diego.

"In science, we can learn about nutrition. And about the chemical properties of food," added Mrs. Braverman. "Why baking powder makes things work, how heat changes the properties of food—that kind of thing."

"How eating a lot makes us healthier," suggested Rocky helpfully.

"These are excellent ideas," said Mr. Haypence. "And you can teach the history of the space program during social studies. Why, there are dozens of ways to tie regular classes in with this project!"

Diego leaned toward Bob. "In gym, we can exercise off all the weight we'll gain from the foods we'll be sampling," he said quietly. Most of the sixth-graders had only just *finished* losing the weight they had gained while they were running their restaurant.

Bob grinned. "And in music, we can sing the theme to *Star Wars*."

"And in art, we can draw pictures of Mr. Frantz to give *us* lots of great thoughts," said Diego.

They smiled at each other. Yes, Mr. Frantz was kind of ridiculous, but this idea of his was going to be great.

"Mr. Haypence, there's that funny man again!" squealed Tiffany as the field-trip buses pulled up in front of the school. "He's standing outside trying to look into your office!"

Startled, Diego glanced out the window. In all the excitement about the space food, he'd forgotten about the weird guy he had seen snooping around the school the day before.

"I don't see anyone, Tiffany," said Mr. Haypence genially. "It wasn't one of the custodians, was it?"

"No! It's that same guy who was spying on

the lunchroom yesterday! He's right—"

Then Tiffany stopped and stared out the window again.

If the man *had* been outside Mr. Haypence's office, he was gone now. There was no one there at all.

Chapter Three
The Great Taste Test

"Hey, Diego! This sounds like something we could use!"

Bob picked up the food catalog he was reading and showed it to Diego. "See?" he said, pointing. "Right here!"

"'Campers' chicken casserole,'" Diego read aloud. "'Contains chicken, potatoes, onions, and carrots—all freeze-dried to keep your backpack as light as possible. One two-ounce package serves twenty people.' Two ounces! Wow! That's incredibly light!"

"Did they take the bones and the gizzards out of the chicken first?" asked Rocky, glancing up from the catalog *he* was reading.

Jennifer Stevens shuddered. "Rocky, do you have to be so gross?"

"I'm not being gross! I'm just wondering how

they get chicken casserole for twenty people to weigh two ounces!"

"It's freeze-dried," Bob explained. "That way you can carry it to the campsite easily. You add water when it's time to cook it, and it kind of turns back into regular food."

"Kind of?" said Rocky suspiciously. "What *is* freeze-drying, anyway?"

"It's a way of preserving foods," said Diego. "You spray the food with some kind of preservative and freeze it. Then you put it in a vacuum chamber and heat it. When it melts, the vacuum sort of sucks away the melting ice crystals until the food is all dried up."

"So what's the point?" asked Rocky suspiciously.

"Well, the food keeps for a long time, and it's really light and easy to pack. Just the kind of thing astronauts aboard a space station would need! You're right, Bob—that's the direction we should be going in."

"I don't know," said Rocky. "I bet that vacuum chamber sucks away a lot of the taste, too. I think we should try to come up with something else. Anyone who's in space for a whole month isn't going to want to eat dried chicken more than once."

Mrs. Doubleday's class was studying English. Only since Project Space Food was underway, today's "English" class meant reading food catalogs and books about space travel instead of learning about punctuation. Mrs. Doubleday was correcting papers at her desk. "I know you can handle looking at catalogs without my help," she had told them at the beginning of the class.

The food catalogs were supposed to give the class ideas. And as far as Diego was concerned, they were doing exactly that.

"I never knew you could freeze-dry so many things!" he marveled as he handed Bob's catalog back. "Chicken casserole, chili, spaghetti... I wonder what it would taste like if you just ate it straight out of the bag without adding water. Hey, maybe we should order some of this stuff to see if we could make something like it!"

Again Rocky looked doubtful. "Why would we want to do that?"

"Well, because we might be able to do even better! I mean, maybe we could make a freeze-dried casserole that weighs only *one* ounce!"

"Doesn't sound like much fun," said Rocky. "And I seem to remember that we were supposed to be coming up with a food that's *fun*. Right?"

"Oh, that was just a guideline," said Diego. confidently. "I bet Mr. Frantz really meant the food is supposed to be interesting."

Rocky picked up his catalog with a sigh. "Well, you're the boss, I guess."

Only a day had passed since the sixth-graders had met Mr. Frantz (if you could really call it meeting him). And already everyone seemed to agree that Diego was in charge of the space-food project. They hadn't taken a vote on it or anything, but people kept *acting* as though he was in charge.

Diego didn't mind, of course. In fact, it made everything easier. He had so many opinions about the kind of space food they should make that he didn't want someone else telling him what to do. And he was so good at scientific stuff like this. He really was the logical choice.

"How's that book, Bonnie?" he asked now. Bonnie was reading a book called *What It's Like to Be an Astronaut.*

"It's good," Bonnie assured him. "It tells you everything about the way astronauts eat nowadays."

"Out of toothpaste tubes, right?" asked Bob.

"Not anymore," said Bonnie. "That's what they used to do. Now they eat pretty regular stuff, except that everything's different when there's no gravity. Like they can't let go of their sandwiches or the whole sandwich will float apart. And they can't pour liquids when they're weightless—the stuff just stays in the container—so they always have to use straws to drink. They actually do eat lots of freeze-dried stuff. And they have so many little packets of food that they have to have scissors at their meals to open them with."

"Hey, forget scissors!" scoffed Louie Watson. "I think those toothpaste tubes sound like a lot more fun. Wouldn't you rather eat something you could squish out of a tube?"

"Totally," agreed Louie's twin brother Larry. "And forget trying to keep the food from floating apart, too. Who wants a regular old boring sandwich that stays where it is?"

The Watson twins were known around school as the Human Demolition Team. They *loved* making messes, and they were amazingly good at it.

"Well, you'd like this, guys," said Bonnie. "This book says that gloppier stuff works better, too—it sticks better to the astronauts' silverware." She held up a picture of a smiling astronaut pointing to a forkful of gummy-looking macaroni and cheese.

"Was that freeze-dried, too?" asked Rocky.

"Yes. They add water just before they serve it."

"Great!" said Rocky sarcastically. "Remind me not to become an astronaut. I'd probably barf to death."

"Well, Rocky, astronauts probably don't care as much about what they eat as you do," Diego reminded him. "They're scientists, remember. They're interested in how *efficient* the food is, not how it tastes,"

Rocky opened his mouth to protest, but Diego swept right on. "I think we should go ahead and order all this freeze-dried stuff so we can study it," he said. "If they send it overnight mail we'll have it by Monday. Mr. Frantz will pay for it, of course. We can have a taste test in the lunchroom, and—"

"Excuse me, students!"

Everyone looked up to see Mr. Haypence smiling in at them. "Hard at work on the space project, I see," he said. "Well, I won't disturb you. I just wanted to take a minute to introduce you to our new substitute teacher, Mr. Chaney. Say hello, class."

"EEEEEEEEEEEEEEEEEEEEK!" screamed Tiffany.

The new substitute teacher was the geeky blond guy who had been snooping around the school.

A substitute teacher! thought Diego. *Then why was he acting so sneaky?*

Mr. Chaney didn't look anything like a teacher. He was peering around curiously, as though he'd never seen a classroom before in his life. His eyes kept darting over to the open catalogs on peoples' desks with much more than normal substitute-teacher interest.

But Mr. Haypence didn't seem to have noticed any of those things. "Why, Tiffany! What kind of a welcome is that?" he asked in a shocked voice.

Tiffany pointed a trembling finger at Mr. Chaney. "But he's ... but he's ... but he's ..." she stammered.

"He's our new substitute for Ms. Burbank," Mr. Haypence filled in. Ms. Burbank was the music teacher, who was about to have a baby. "I know we're *all* going to make every effort to welcome him to Hollis." And he gave Tiffany a meaningful stare.

Then he patted Mr. Chaney on the shoulder. "I've got to get back to the office now," he said. "Why don't you hang around a little, get acquainted with everybody?" And with another meaningful stare at Tiffany, Mr. Haypence left the room.

"I wonder why Mr. Chaney doesn't want to

hang around the music room instead?" Diego whispered to Bob.

"Maybe he thinks we're more interesting," Bob whispered back. "Don't *you*?"

Mrs. Doubleday also seemed a little startled at having an unexpected guest, but she put down her pen and smiled. "You're welcome to spend as much time with us as you want," she said. "As you can see, the kids are getting some ideas for their space-food project. Did Mr. Haypence fill you in on that?"

"He certainly did. It sounds very interesting," said Mr. Chaney eagerly.

He was standing right next to Bob's desk. Now he leaned over Bob's shoulder. "Camping supplies?" he asked in a puzzled voice.

"Oh, we're just trying to come up with some ideas," Bob said.

Mr. Chaney peered more closely at the catalog. "And what are some of the ideas you've come up with so far?" he wanted to know.

Before Bob could open his mouth, Diego answered for him. "We haven't really come up with anything specific," he said quickly. "We're still kind of in the planning stages."

"I see." Mr. Chaney looked disappointed. "Well, be sure to let me know when you've come up with some ideas, won't you?"

"Of course we will," said Diego.

But inside he was saying, *Of course we won't.*

Because if Mr. Chaney was supposed to be a music teacher, why wasn't he in the music room? And why was a music teacher so interested in space food anyway? And why had he been snooping around in the first place?

Maybe I'm acting too much like Tiffany, thought Diego. *But I think Mr. Chaney really is a spy.*

And Diego couldn't see any reason to tell him anything at all.

"Here's some more freeze-dried food!" called Diego as he strode into the lunchroom with a huge box on his shoulder. "Boy, they weren't kidding. This stuff really *is* light! Here, catch!" And he tossed the box to Bob as easily as if it had been a pack of Kleenex.

Bob slit the tape on the boxes. Then he pulled out the foil packets inside and lined them up on a lunchroom table.

Beef stew. Chicken fricassee. Franks 'n' beans.

"You'd think hot dogs wouldn't need to be freeze-dried," commented Bob. "I mean, they've got so much weird stuff in them already that they should keep forever."

34

Diego pulled out another packet labeled MAC-
ARONI AND CHEESE. Then came packets of chili
and roast duck in orange sauce.

"That's probably for special occasions," said
Jennifer Stevens. "You know, romantic candle-
lit dinners."

"Are astronauts allowed to burn candles in
space?" asked Jonathan Matterhorn. "Seems a
little risky, somehow."

"Oh, I'm sure they can get permission from
ground control if they're really in love," said
Jennifer.

Dessert packets came next. There was freeze-
dried apple brown Betty. Chocolate pudding.
Chocolate ice cream. ("Freeze-dried *ice cream?*"
said Chantilly Lace.) Pineapple nut cake.
Oatmeal-raisin crisp. . . .

"You know what?" said Rocky. "This stuff
sounds like *lunchroom* food!"

"Oh, it'll be a lot better than that," Diego
promised him. "The technology for this stuff has
really improved."

He was slicing open the packet of beef stew
as he spoke. Now he shook it eagerly into one
of the bowls on the table.

Out came a few dusty-looking brown lumps
and a handful of brownish powder.

"Yeah," said Rocky after a second. "I can see
what you mean."

"Well, you have to add water!" said Diego. He dashed out to the kitchen and poured two cups of hot water into the bowl. Then he gave it a quick stir and returned to his friends.

"See?" he said. "It's a lot better when . . ."

His voice trailed off. The lumps, powder, and water had blended together the way they were supposed to. But somehow they didn't look a whole lot like the kind of beef stew Diego's parents made. It didn't smell like it, either.

"Who wants to try some?" Diego asked.

There was a ringing silence in the lunchroom.

"Oh, come on, you guys! We're supposed to be scientific about this!"

But no one in the lunchroom seemed to feel very scientific that day.

"Well, if no one else will try it, I will," Diego announced. And he scraped a big forkful of stew out of the bowl. *I'm a scientist,* he told himself silently, *and scientists do not hold their noses when they're taste-testing.*

It tasted quite a lot like salt. Wet, mushy salt with some stringy chunks of salt floating in it. It was so salty, in fact, that Diego forgot to worry about its smell.

Diego put the fork down gently. Then he glanced at the rest of the foil packets waiting on the table.

Everyone was watching him. "So what do you think?" asked Chantilly.

"Let me try that duck," said Diego.

The duck wasn't quite as salty as the stew. On the other hand, its burned-rubber taste wasn't much of an improvement. Not to mention that it smelled like the Indy 500.

The apple brown Betty wasn't salty at all. It even smelled kind of nice, like cinnamon. But it sure didn't taste good—not unless you *liked* eating blobs of rubbery sugar with dried-up apple pellets in it.

"Okay," said Diego. He pushed the bowl away and stood up.

"As Mr. Haypence said, the eyes of the world are upon us," he announced. "And now that we've had this taste test—or I have, anyway—I think our mission is clear.

"We've *got* to come up with something that's better than this gross-out garbage."

Chapter Four

Take Twenty
Junior Mints...

"And, uh, what do you usually do in music class?" asked Mr. Chaney.

"Okay," muttered Diego under his breath, "there's one *more* thing you don't know."

Today was the first time Mrs. Doubleday's class had actually had Mr. Chaney as a substitute in music. And Diego was becoming more and more certain that Mr. Chaney was no ordinary substitute music teacher. Or any kind of teacher at all.

There was the way he played the piano, for instance—or tried to. Diego had never seen a music teacher who plonked the keys with one finger and *still* missed half the notes. Mr. Chaney didn't seem to know how to read music, either. (Diego wasn't a great musician, but at least he knew which end of the sheet music was right-side-up. Mr. Chaney had been holding his upside-down for the past fifteen minutes.) And Mr. Chaney couldn't tell the difference between the sixth-graders and the kindergarteners, either. "Shall we sing, uh, 'Ring Around the Rosy'?" he had asked at the beginning of class a few minutes ago.

Suddenly Diego realized that no one in the class had answered Mr. Chaney's question about what they did in music class. He decided to give the substitute a little test.

"Mostly we discuss the world's major symphonies," he told Mr. Chaney solemnly. "Which one is *your* favorite?"

Mr. Chaney looked faintly alarmed. "Well, of course I like almost *all* the major symphonies," he said after a second. "But I guess I'd have to say that, uh, Beethoven is my favorite symphony writer."

"You mean composer?" asked Diego. *Everyone's heard of Beethoven,* he was thinking. "And who's your favorite modern composer?"

Mr. Chaney bit his lip. "Gee, I would have an awfully hard time picking one over the others," he faltered. "I mean, they're all so good that—" Suddenly he broke off. "I tell you what, guys! Let's take a break from music today, shall we? I never liked music when I was your age. Let's talk about something else."

"Like what?" asked Junior Smith in surprise.

"Oh, anything," said Mr. Chaney. "Anything you want!"

"How about the stock exchange?" suggested Junior.

"Well, maybe not the stock exchange," said Mr. Chaney. Then he leaned forward. "How about your space-food project? How is it coming along?" he asked eagerly. "I'd be happy to talk about that, if you want."

What is going on here? wondered Diego.

Actually, the space-food project was coming along fine. Everyone in the sixth grade had lots of ideas, and most of them spent all their free time experimenting in the lunchroom. Since Diego was *definitely* in charge of things now, it was his job to supervise the experiments.

Not everyone wanted him to supervise them, of course. One afternoon, when Diego wandered over to Bonnie and Chantilly's corner of the lunchroom, they both screamed and hurled themselves protectively over the lunch table.

"GET AWAY! DON'T LOOK! IT'S TOO STUPID!"

Then Bonnie got hold of herself again. "We don't really have anything to show you, anyway," she said, smoothing her hair. "We've just been kind of, you know, taking notes."

But she and Chantilly both stayed hunched over the table.

"Oh, come on, you nuts," said Diego tolerantly. "You've been working away in this corner like crazy for the past two days. You must have come up with *something.*"

"Well, if you really have to know, we've been making these," said Chantilly. And slowly she stood up to show him.

"These" were a row of flat, wizened, shriveled apple pies. They looked like regular pies with the air let out of them.

"Hey, neat!" said Diego. "What are they?"

"They're supposed to be freeze-dried apple pies," Bonnie said bitterly. "Only I guess we didn't quite get the freeze-drying part right."

Now Diego felt totally confused. "But I thought we weren't going to do freeze-dried stuff!" he said.

"We weren't," said Bonnie, "but we couldn't come up with *anything* else. So we started thinking."

"We wondered if maybe the reason that that freeze-dried stuff from the catalogs was so bad was that it wasn't made well in the first place," Chantilly added. "We decided that something homemade would taste a lot better. The thing is, we weren't quite sure how to freeze-dry stuff on our own."

"How did you do it?" asked Diego. *Don't let me start smiling,* he prayed. *They'll get too mad at me.*

"Well, we *thought* we'd done it the way you said," Bonnie told him. "We baked the pies—it was my mother's recipe—and sprayed them with a preservative."

"We didn't exactly know what kind of preservative to use," Chantilly confessed. "So we just sprayed some hairspray on them. Hairspray is like a preservative, isn't it? And we didn't see how just a tiny bit of it could be poisonous. Then we froze the pies. Then we wanted to do the heat-in-a-vacuum part, only we weren't sure how."

Bonnie took up the story again. "So we put them in an oven and set it on warm and—oh, this is going to sound so stupid!—we stuck a vacuum-cleaner hose in there and turned it on for a couple of hours."

"You didn't," said Diego.

Bonnie nodded miserably. "I *told* you it was stupid," she said. "Plus my mother's kind of mad at me for melting her vacuum-cleaner hose."

"W-well, it's not stupid, exactly," said Diego,

"only that's not the way you make a vacuum chamber." He couldn't help smiling a little. "I don't really think freeze-drying is something that can be done at home, guys. But maybe it's for the best. That hairspray might have turned out to be a problem."

If Bonnie and Chantilly had gotten off the track a little, some other kids in the sixth grade had never really been *on* the track. The Watson twins hadn't even come close to thinking up a new food yet. They were too busy with what they called their "road tests." He'd only felt like *smiling* when he'd found out what Bonnie and Chantilly were up to. When he saw the twins' "'experiments,'" he nearly cracked up.

The twins did their road tests at home, where Diego visited them one afternoon. Road tests meant putting food in the road to see how well it could stand up to being run over. "After all, conditions in space can get pretty intense," Louie Watson explained. "You never know when an asteroid might bang into the space station or something. We don't want to waste our time coming up with a food that's just going to crumble all over the cabin."

He was busy tying a rope around a loaf of bread as he spoke. "That's why we're doing this," he said. He looked both ways to make sure no cars were coming down the street. Then he darted out to the middle of the road, placed the loaf of bread carefully in the middle, and darted back to his front yard.

"I hear a car," Larry shouted a couple of minutes later. "Here it comes! Get back behind the bushes so they don't see us!"

The three boys ducked behind the bushes as the car passed by. When it was safely out of sight, Louie reeled in the loaf of bread excitedly.

"Oops," he said after a second. "I guess bread doesn't stand up to the road test. Not even pumpernickel, like this."

"Well, let's not get discouraged," said Larry. "It looks a lot better than the meat loaf we tried yesterday."

Diego decided to leave them to it. All in all, it was probably better to keep the twins as far away from the kitchen as possible. At least the road tests would distract them for a while.

Tiffany's house wasn't too far from the Watsons', so Diego decided to stop by and see how she was doing before he went home for supper. He found her fretting in the kitchen.

"It's so hard to figure out how to protect your food!" she said in a worried voice.

"Protect it?" echoed Diego. "Protect it from what? Germs?"

"No, no. Germs aren't the problem. I'm thinking about all the stuff that could happen in space! What if aliens break into the space station and *laser* the food? Do you think it would work if I made some kind of ray deflector out of aluminum foil?"

Diego couldn't help it. He burst out laughing.

"Do you honestly think that's going to happen, Tiffany?" he asked. "And even if it did, do you really think the astronauts would be worried about their *food*?"

"Well, maybe not," Tiffany admitted. Then her forehead furrowed with concern again. "But what if the *Orion* goes too close to the sun, and all the food gets overcooked?"

"Sorry, Tiff, but that's not something I can help you with," said Diego. "I tell you what, though. You and the Watson twins might like to work together on this project. You're on kind of the same wavelength."

Back in the lunchroom the next day, Diego found Jennifer Stevens knotted up over a different problem.

"Have you seen any pictures of the *Orion*? It's so ugly inside!" she complained. "How can those astronauts *stand* it? I want my food to have eye appeal."

"Eye appeal?"

"Yes. You know, like, be good-looking. Otherwise those poor astronauts are going to go out of their minds. I sure would, staring at all that stupid-looking science equipment. Whatever I come up with has to put, like, *beauty* into their lives."

Junior Smith wasn't worried about eye appeal. "I think this whole space thing is a total waste of money," he said angrily when Diego stopped by his table. "Billions and billions of taxpayers' dollars, for what? Just so some guys in puffy suits can joyride around outer space for a month!"

This was the kind of statement that drove Diego crazy.

"They're doing research," he told Junior tensely. "It may pay off someday. And even if it doesn't, space exploration isn't the kind of thing you should cut corners on!

"Sorry to sound so preachy," Diego added in his regular voice. "I get a little carried away sometimes. So have you decided not to come up with a space food after all?"

"Oh, no. I'm still working on one. I'm just trying to figure out how to make a *cheap* one."

Diego looked more closely at the items piled up on Junior's table. There were a few Styrofoam cups, a coil of rope, an old plastic sandwich wrapper, and an empty brown-sugar box.

"I get it," he said. "You're trying to figure out what to put your food in. And these things are here to give you some ideas about how to package it."

"No way!" said Junior. He sounded amazed that Diego could be so wrong. "These things are going to be part of the food! I'm trying to save the taxpayers money, remember. And if I can figure out a way to make food out of stuff like this, I'm going to save a *lot* of money."

Especially since no one will go near your food, thought Diego as he made his escape. *NASA can reuse it for every voyage.*

He was starting to feel a little depressed. None of his friends had come up with anything that seemed right for the *Orion*. And the time was slipping by so fast!

Diego glanced around the lunchroom. Rocky was sitting at a table in the corner and scribbling furiously away. There was a huge pile of candy in front of him—brain food, Diego guessed. At least whatever *Rocky* was working on would involve real food. Diego decided to pay him a visit.

"Oh, hi!" Rocky greeted him. "You know, I was starting to worry that I'd never come up with a decent idea. And now all of a sudden I've got millions of them!"

He shoved a pile of paper over at Diego. "I've been writing recipes," he said proudly. "Which one do you think sounds the best? I have some samples here if you want."

Diego began to read the recipe on the top of the heap. It was called mint-mallow delight. "Take twenty Junior Mints," it began. "Spear them with toothpicks. Then spear twenty miniature marshmallows and . . ."

Diego looked down at the table. Yes, there were twenty skewers of mint-mallow delight. He flipped quickly to the second recipe—cherry chewies: Melt three packs of cherry Life Savers in a glass of hot lemonade. Add one cup cherry-flavored Jujyfruits, stir until thick, and mold into squares. . . .

The next recipe involved dipping Sugar Babies into chocolate syrup and freezing them. (Sugar bullets, the recipe was called.) And the one after that—fruit fiestas—had something to do with combining tropical-fruit-flavored gumdrops and regular-fruit-flavored taffy.

Diego dropped the sheaf of recipes in horror. Had everyone in the sixth grade lost their mind except for him?

"So what do you think?" asked Rocky. "It's hard to decide which one to choose, isn't it?"

"Rocky, we can't send a bunch of *candy* into orbit!" Diego exploded.

"Why not?" protested Rocky. "People like candy!"

"Ordinary people, maybe," said Diego. "But astronauts aren't ordinary people. They're scientists! We have to give them something interesting, not something they're going to laugh at!"

Rocky jumped to his feet. "You think these recipes are silly and ridiculous? Well, I think *you're* being stupid, Diego! No one asked you to be in charge of this project! And your ideas are totally wrong this time!"

Purple-faced with fury, Rocky shuffled his recipes into a stack and stormed out of the lunchroom.

Diego sighed as he watched Rocky slam the lunchroom door behind him.

Okay, maybe I was a little too hard on him, he said to himself. *Maybe I was acting too bossy. But I know I'm right—and anyway, I'll make it up to him tomorrow.*

But the next day Rocky was sitting sulkily at a completely empty lunch table.

Diego forced himself to go over to him. "Hey, where are your experiments?" he asked in as nice a voice as he could manage.

"I ate them," Rocky replied shortly.

Chapter Five

Rocky's Revolt

"I won't! I won't! I won't try another bite!"

Lucy Wu, a fifth-grader, was the one doing the shouting.

"Oh, come on, Lucy," coaxed Jennifer Stevens. "Just one tiny spoonful. See how pretty it is?" She held out a spoon filled with bright pink bubbles.

"I'm *tired* of trying space food!" Lucy yelled. "You can't make me eat any more!"

Ever since Mr. Haypence had volunteered the fifth-graders to be space-food testers, rebellion had been quietly simmering in the fifth grade. Now, all of a sudden, things weren't so quiet anymore.

It was Jennifer's pink, bubbly Flower Foam dessert that was causing all the trouble. Up until now, the fifth-graders had been pretty good about trying peoples' inventions. They had patiently swallowed futuristic french fries made of soybeans and prebaked pancakes that the astronauts were supposed to heat by sticking them to one of the space-station windows. Saturn-shaped meat-loaf patties—no problem! Doughnuts baked around flashlights—fine!

But even the most goody-goodyish of the fifth-graders wouldn't touch Jennifer's Flower Foam.

"It doesn't look like food!" Lucy Wu complained.

"It's not *supposed* to!" said Jennifer indignantly. "It's supposed to make the astronauts' meals prettier! Besides, it tastes okay! It's not, like, the best thing you've ever eaten, but it won't make you sick!"

"Yes, it will," promised Lucy Wu. She clamped her mouth shut and turned her head away like a toddler rejecting a spoonful of pureed squash. And neither she nor the rest of the fifth-graders would taste any more space food after that.

The fifth-graders' strike was only the most recent of Diego's problems. Three more days had passed, and none of the sixth-graders had yet managed to come up with a food that Diego thought was worth sending on the *Orion*.

"How's it going, kids?" called Mr. Haypence

at lunchtime. He glanced approvingly around the lunchroom. Every table was filled with kids eating their lunches while they worked on their space-food projects. "Have you decided what the astronauts are going to be eating, Diego?"

Diego gave him a thin smile. "Hot dogs and potato chips, if we don't find something pretty fast," he said.

"Oh, don't be so hard on yourself!" said Mr. Haypence. "You'll make the deadline without *any* trouble. Remember, the eyes of the world are upon you!"

Somehow that didn't fill Diego with confidence.

"I trust you implicitly, Diego," said Mr. Haypence as he walked out. "I know you're going to bring Hollis all the glory it deserves."

Diego sighed. "Thanks for stopping by to cheer me up," he muttered gloomily.

A girl named Cindi Melcher, who had overheard all this, gave a wounded sniff. "You wouldn't be having so much trouble if you'd just go ahead and pick my food the way I keep telling you to," she said.

Not this again, thought Diego. Cindi had already changed her project three times. And each time she had ignored the fact that there was no gravity inside the space station.

"Cindi, I thought the scrambled eggs tasted great," he told her patiently. (Actually, they had tasted terrible. Cindi had mixed them with bacon bits, crushed toast, grape jelly, and instant-coffee granules. "I call it Breakfast-Pak," she had explained.) "But scrambled eggs are too hard to eat in outer space. They don't stick to a fork."

"So the astronauts have to chase them around a little bit!" said Cindi. "It's good exercise!"

"Don't bother trying to convince him, Cindi," Junior put in. "He said no to my Econo-Lunch, too." Econo-Lunch was the one made out of melted Styrofoam cups and generic peanut butter. "He said *all* of it had to be edible, not just part," Junior added in disgust. "He didn't even care how much money I was saving! So the next time your tax bill comes to a zillion dollars, you can just blame Diego."

"I will," said Cindi. Then she turned to Diego. "If you're such an expert on space food, why haven't *you* come up with an idea of your own?" she demanded. "Maybe if you knew how hard it was to think of something, you wouldn't just go around stamping on *other* people's food!"

"Well, Diego, it seems to me that was a good question," said Diego's mother that night at supper. "Why *haven't* you come up with an idea of your own?"

"Oh, I have," Diego assured her. "I just wanted to hold back for a little while."

"But why, when your deadline is so close?" asked Mr. Lopez.

"Well, this sounds kind of conceited, but..." Diego's voice trailed off. "But I think my idea's so good that it will probably be the one to be picked. So I kind of wanted to wait around and see if anyone else might come up with something good first. I mean, if I'm in charge of this whole thing, don't you think I should kind of keep out of the race until I *have* to get in it?"

"No! That doesn't make any sense!" said Diego's father. "If you were running for president, you'd vote for yourself, wouldn't you?"

"Well, sure, but—"

"I don't see why this is any different," said Mrs. Lopez. "If your idea's really the best, that's the way it is! You don't have to hold off just because you're in charge of the project.

"Besides, you don't *know* that your idea's going to be the best," she reminded him gently. "And even if it's not the one that's picked, it will still be worth it. The point is to use your mind to come up with the best possible idea— no matter whose it is."

Carlos, Diego's younger brother, had been silent during this discussion. Now he looked up from his plate.

"If Diego becomes president, can I have his telescope?"

"Okay," said Diego happily. "Now you can help me put in the shortening." He pushed an empty bowl and a can of white, gunky shortening across the table to Chantilly.

Chantilly eyed it with distaste. "Remind me again why we're using shortening," she said.

"We need something with a lot of calories," said Diego. "If we can come up with a food that has all the calories a person needs in a whole day, that means the astronauts will only have to eat once a day!"

Chantilly nodded. "And, um, remind me again why we only want them to eat once a day." she said.

"Because they've got so much work to do up there," Diego explained. "If they can get away with one meal a day, they'll be able to work a lot harder."

"But what if they think they're working hard enough already?" asked Chantilly reasonably. "What if they *want* to take a lunch break?"

"Oh, that's not the way scientists think," said Diego. "Look at me. When *I'm* doing an experiment, I hate having to keep stopping to eat."

Chantilly said no more.

It was the day after Diego's suppertime talk with his parents. School had just let out, and Diego and Chantilly were working together in the lunchroom.

"You put in a cup of that stuff," Diego directed Chantilly. "I'll stir in the pulverized vitamin pills and brewer's yeast."

Wincing, Chantilly scraped a big blob of greasy white goop against the side of the bowl. "Ugh!" she said with a shudder. "It's so slimy!" She poked the shortening into the bowl with a spoon while Diego poured in a cupful of chewable vitamins that had been crushed to a powder and mixed with a smelly brown powder (the brewer's yeast).

"There," he said with satisfaction. "Now the astronauts will have all the vitamins they need, too."

The shortening was a sticky white mass. Mixed with the vitamins, it turned a pale orange—sort of like the color of baby aspirin. "Hey, that doesn't look so bad!" said Chantilly.

"Yeah, but we still have to add the powdered milk," Diego reminded her. "We need that to bring the protein level up to what an astronaut would need for a whole day. And we've got to add the bran, too, to give our food enough fiber.

"This stuff probably won't be that good-looking," Diego went on. "But I guarantee it's going to be the most nutritious food the astronauts will ever have tasted."

"*If* they can stand to even taste it," said Chantilly under her breath. "I can't even stand to look at it."

"Wait till you try these!" said Diego. "You won't need to eat anything else today!"

And he held out a plate of flat, lumpy, grayish disks.

Everyone looked, but no one spoke. After a while, Bob took a deep breath. "Looks interesting," he said. "What are they?"

"I call them Totally Food Wafers," Diego told him. "I made them last night."

Diego had finished the Totally Food Wafers while the rest of Pasadena—including Chantilly—was eating supper. ("*You* may hate eating during an experiment," she had told him as she left, "but I don't.") He had divided the mass of grayish dough into twenty-five equal portions—one for everyone in Mrs. Doubleday's class, including Mrs. Doubleday. Then he had shaped the dough into lumps about the size of a doughnut, flattened them, and baked them in the lunchroom's microwave.

"Each wafer provides a full day's nutrition," Diego said proudly. "All the calories, all the vitamins, all the minerals, all the protein— everything you need for the whole day. If you eat one of these now, you won't need to waste any time on lunch *or* supper!"

Despite this ringing endorsement, no one in Mrs. Doubleday's class rushed forward to grab a Totally Food Wafer off the plate.

"Have you had one?" asked Bonnie cautiously.

"I sure have," Diego said. "I had one for supper last night, hot off the baking sheet. It was deli—"

Suddenly Diego stopped. He had been about to say, "It was delicious." But that wasn't exactly true. The Totally Food Wafers were incredibly gross tasting. If you swallowed them down fast, though, you could get the taste out of your mouth pretty easily with a few quarts of cherry soda.

"They taste quite interesting," Diego corrected himself. "Come on, guys, try one! You won't believe how unhungry you'll feel for the rest of the day!"

"Oh, yes, I will," Diego thought he heard someone—was it Rocky?—whisper.

"*I'd* love to try one," said Mrs. Doubleday firmly. "I think it was very innovative of you, Diego."

And she lifted the first Totally Food Wafer off the plate.

Slowly, reluctantly Diego's classmates followed Mrs. Doubleday's example. Slowly, reluctantly they lifted their Totally Food Wafers to their mouths and took a bite. Slowly, and with expressions of loathing, they chewed, chewed, chewed, and chewed some more.

"They're a little tough," Diego said. "Do you think I baked them too long, Chantilly?"

"Oh, no!" said Chantilly fervently. "I-I'd rather have them kind of dry, I think."

"Yeah," agreed Rocky. "If they were wet, I might worry that I was eating some kind of squishy swamp creature."

Diego chuckled. "I know they're not as good as cheeseburgers, Rocky," he said. "But they're a hundred times better for you. Literally."

"No one's hungry yet, right?" Diego asked a couple of hours later.

"No," the class groaned.

"No one wants lunch, right?" he asked a couple of hours after that.

No, no one wanted lunch.

"These are really a pretty great invention, don't you think?" Diego couldn't help asking half an hour before school let out. He didn't want to brag, but he was so proud he couldn't help it. "I mean, we've been sitting in this classroom the whole day, and *still* no one's hungry!"

"It's amazing," said Chantilly glumly.

"So what do you think, guys?" asked Diego. "Don't you think Totally Food Wafers would be a great food for the astronauts to take aboard the *Orion*?"

There was a silence. "You don't have to decide today," said Diego quickly. "You can tell me tomorrow if you want."

Bob sighed. "I guess we should go with the Totally Food Wafers," he said. "They were a good idea."

"And they're cheap," chimed in Junior Smith sadly.

"And you *are* a genius, after all," said Tiffany.

Diego looked quizzically around the room. No one else said anything.

"Great!" he said, and jumped to his feet. "I'll go call Mr. Frantz and tell him we're ready to go!"

"Hang on a minute, Diego."

It was Rocky. And was it Diego's imagination or did he sound a little . . . steely?

"Diego," he said coldly, "why did Mr. Frantz ask us kids to come up with a food?"

"Because he knew we were qualified, I guess," said Diego. "I mean, with the science fair and everything—"

"That's not why."

Rocky slowly stood up. He slowly walked toward Diego. When his face was about six inches away from Diego's nose, he slowly opened his mouth.

"The reason Mr. Frantz asked us to come up with this food was that he wanted a *fun* food!" he shouted. "He didn't want some terrible-tasting, good-for-you glop! You're acting worse than . . . than Ms. Weinstock! No one *cares* about food that's really nutritious if it tastes like barf!"

"Wait a minute!" said Diego.

"No, *you* wait a minute!" shouted Rocky. "You've practically *railroaded* this class into going along with your TOTALLY STUPID WAFERS! Without even taking a vote or *anything*! It's . . . it's UNAMERICAN! Just because you're a so-called genius doesn't mean you're always right, you know!" Rocky's face was dark red and he was huffing, he was so angry.

"But I—" Diego began.

Rocky just drowned out whatever Diego was

going to say. "It's practically unpatriotic to give chunks of garbage like your TOTALLY FUNGUS WAFERS to the astronauts!" he hollered, puffing out his chest. "And if you tell Mr. Frantz that those dried-out lumps of baked grease are the best we could come up with, I'm seceding from the sixth grade!"

To Diego's horror, his classmates all burst into loud cheers. *Now that I think about it,* he thought, *I really feel kind of relieved. Those Totally Food Wafers really did taste like barf!*

Chapter Six

The Space Crystals Are Born

"I hope you're not coming down with something awful," Diego's mother said worriedly. She touched his forehead. "You don't feel feverish."

"I think it's just some kind of twenty-four-hour thing," Diego croaked, collapsing feebly onto his pillow. (Diego might not be a total genius, but he was smart enough to know how to con his way out of school.) "I'm sure I'll be better tomorrow."

"Hmmm," his mother said, eyeing him. *Uh-oh,* Diego thought, *did I overdo it?* Mrs. Lopez looked at her watch. "Well, I've already called the school to tell them you won't be coming in today. I guess a day of rest will be good for you. You take it easy, okay? I better get going." She was in a rush because she'd just spent about a half-hour writing a long list of emergency phone numbers for Diego. She worried about leaving him alone. She gave Diego a kiss and hurried out the door.

Diego lay in bed, listening to his mother start the car. When she was safely out of the garage and down the street, he counted to twenty. (Just to be even safer.) Then he leapt out of bed, raced to the phone, and punched in Rocky's number.

"Hello?" Rocky answered hoarsely. Then he coughed a few times.

"She's gone," Diego told him.

"Great! So's mine!" Rocky said in his normal voice. "I'll be right over."

Rocky wasn't going to secede from the sixth grade after all. Instead, he and Diego were going to spend the day developing a totally new space food. On their own.

Once everyone had agreed that Totally Food Wafers were a total mistake, they'd gone back to the drawing board, or in their case, back to the lunchroom laboratory. The problem was, everyone had used up all their best ideas already. After two days of trying stuff that was even worse than Totally Food Wafers, Diego and Rocky had hatched a secret plan.

They would work together, combining Rocky's

food expertise with Diego's scientific knowledge. Away from the distractions of the lunchroom and their classmates, working in Diego's kitchen, they would create the ultimate space food. Diego's own science equipment was just as good as the stuff Mr. Haypence had set up in the lunchroom, anyway. In fact, it was even better.

Diego and Rocky didn't want their classmates to feel that they were holding out on them, though. So that was why Diego was letting a furtive-looking Rocky into his house twenty minutes later.

"Your parents won't be back all day, right?" he asked Rocky.

"Right," said Rocky. "No sweat. I'm home-free until dinnertime."

"Not that our parents would mind if they knew what we were doing," Diego said. "It's not really playing hooky, after all. We're doing something for our country. Still, let's make sure everything is cleaned up and you're out of here before *my* parents get home. Come on into the kitchen."

"Wow!" said Rocky appreciatively when he saw the kitchen. "You've been busy!"

Every counter in the kitchen was covered

with bottles and jars and plates of chemicals. Diego had spent all yesterday after school buying them at a scientific supply house. There were murky green liquids and bright-yellow oils. There were bluish granules and pinkish crystals. There was something that looked like uncooked oatmeal, and a little pile of tiny black beads, and more colored powders than Diego and Rocky had ever seen in one place before.

"So this time we're *really* going to poison the astronauts, right?" asked Rocky cheerfully.

"No! Of course not! *All* food has chemicals in it! And everything here is completely edible."

But Rocky just grinned. "I figured that, actually," he said. "I was just teasing you."

Diego had also brought in a Bunsen burner—"It will be more fun to use than the stove," he said—and all the gleaming utensils from his chemistry set which he'd never used because he had forgotten it was under his bed. And of course there was another jar of multicolored chewable vitamins.

"Whatever we make might as well still be good for you," he said to Rocky.

"Fine," Rocky agreed. "Just as long as no one can tell. What are we going to use all these chemicals for, anyway?"

"We don't know yet," said Diego. "It's your

job to decide what you want our space food to be like. It's my job to make sure it comes out that way."

"Great!" said Rocky. "But before I can start thinking about space food, I've got to think about real food. I'm starving. What do you have in this kitchen that *isn't* a pure chemical?"

"Chantilly, hold out your hand," said Diego in the lunchroom on Monday.

"Why? Are you asking her to go steady?" asked Jennifer with interest.

Everyone at the surrounding tables turned around to stare.

"No, of course I'm not!" said Diego. He could feel his face turning hot. "I just want to show her something."

"It's not a lizard or anything like that, is it?" asked Chantilly suspiciously.

"No. It's Rocky's and my new space food," said Diego.

"It sounds truly scary," Chantilly said, but she still held out her hand.

From behind his back Diego pulled out a salt-shaker. Carefully he shook a few tiny white crystals into Chantilly's hand.

"*Salt?*" said Chantilly. "You want to give the astronauts *salt?*"

Then she gasped. "Wait a minute! What's happening?"

The tiny crystals were starting to jump around. Then they exploded in the palm of her hand—and before her astonished eyes they burst into a rainbow assortment of glittering crystals the size of popcorn.

"How beautiful!" exclaimed Chantilly. "What *are* they?"

"They're Space Crystals," said Rocky. He was beaming like a proud father. "And they're more than beautiful. Taste one."

"Look how shiny they are!" marveled Chantilly, and she picked up a pink crystal and put it into her mouth.

A smile lit up her face. "Hey, it's peach flavored!" she said. "No, wait! Chocolate! No, caramel! No, lemon! Wait a minute! The flavors keep changing!"

"That's right," said Diego happily. "For as long as it's in your mouth, the flavors will keep changing. And five crystals have a whole day's worth of vitamins and minerals."

Rocky had persuaded Diego that there was no point in having the crystals replace regular meals. "People *like* regular meals," he had explained. "Our space food will just be like the icing on the cake. It's something *extra* for the

astronauts. It's fun to eat *and* good for you, and they can have it whenever they want—as dessert or as a snack. Speaking of snacks..."

"I picked the flavors," Rocky said now. "Diego talked me out of having one of them be pizza, though."

"How do they explode like that?" asked Bob.

"They're heat activated," Diego told him. "They need to be in a person's hand for a few seconds before they'll work."

"Diego, these are incredible! Can I have some more?" said Chantilly. Bonnie, Jennifer, and even timid Tiffany had enthusiastically eaten the rest of her crystals. ("This is almost too pretty to eat," Jennifer had said. Then, as another kid tried to grab it away from her, she popped it into her mouth. "Wow! These things are totally fabulous!" she'd cried.)

"Hey, wait! I want some!" said a girl at another table.

"Me, too! Me, too!" Suddenly everyone in the lunchroom was swarming around Diego and his saltshaker. And everyone who tried Space Crystals was smiling.

"Well, these are it!" said Bob. "I mean, *this* is it. I mean, these are what we should send with the astronauts. Aren't they awesome?" he exclaimed.

A burst of cheers and cries of "kowabunga!" answered him.

"No, wait! We should take a vote on it!" Diego said quickly.

"We don't have to vote *this* time," said Rocky. "You can see it's unanimous." He leaned over and slapped Diego five. "Nice work, dude! I think we're a winning team!"

"Well, my gosh! What's all this commotion?"

It was Mr. Chaney, and as he pushed his way through the crowd, the lunchroom grew quieter and quieter. It seemed as if everyone was suspicious of the weird new substitute teacher. It was hard to explain why exactly, but no one really trusted him. He was always sneaking up on people, snooping around halls and lockers, always popping up where he was least expected. He was especially interested in the space-food project, and Diego had gradually become convinced that Tiffany was right, for once, to worry so much about Mr. Chaney. He was obviously a *spy!*

"Oh, we're just—just goofing around," said Diego quickly. "Sorry we were making so much noise. Come on, everyone! Let's sit down again!"

"It's just that we're *so excited*" gushed Jennifer. *Shut up, shut up, shut up,* Diego frantically tried to radio his thoughts. "Diego and

71

Rocky's new space food is just so fantastic!"

Well, that did it, Diego thought forlornly. *Leave it to stupid Jennifer to open her stupid big blabbermouth.*

"A new space food? Isn't that exciting!" said Mr. Chaney. "May I see?"

There was no way around it. Slowly Diego shook a few white grains into his hand. And within seconds they had performed their miracle.

Mr. Chaney was ecstatic.

"These are marvelous!" he exclaimed with his mouth full. "The astronauts will love them!"

"They're so gorgeous!" bragged Jennifer happily. "They even taste good. Plus they're full of vitamins."

Mr. Chaney turned to Diego. "These are quite impressive," he said. "What did you say they're called?"

"Space Crystals," said Jennifer before Diego could open his mouth.

While Jennifer had been babbling, Diego had stood by helplessly. *Maybe I should throw myself on her and cover her mouth,* he'd thought. *I could pretend I'm having a fit or something!* But knowing Jennifer, she'd probably think he was trying to *kiss* her or something! Anyway, by the time Diego had thought all this out, Jennifer had just blabbed everything and it was too late.

"Did you really make these yourself?" Mr. Chaney asked.

Diego nodded dumbly.

"Where's the recipe?" the spy wanted to know.

"Oh, I—I don't really write recipes down," said Diego frantically. "We just kind of improvised this. I don't think we could even come up with the same thing again. Do you, Rocky?"

"No way," said Rocky. He'd never liked Mr. Chaney since the day he'd caught him snooping in the lunchroom. "This was just a fluke. A once-in-a-lifetime fluke. Next time we try, I bet they'll taste like mud."

"Don't you believe them!" said Tiffany. *Oh, great,* Diego thought, *everyone's getting blabbermouth disease.* "They're just being modest. Diego's got a photographic memory. He can remember a thing *forever!*"

Diego and Rocky exchanged a look of horror. What a disaster! They were really stuck, now!

But to Diego's relief, Mr. Chaney didn't pursue the recipe question. He just glanced at his watch and said, "Oops! I've got to get back to the music room. The piano tuner will be here any minute." Then he took off.

Diego tried not to think about Mr. Chaney

for the rest of the day. *Maybe if I don't think about him, he'll go away,* he thought lamely. But when he was walking out to the bike rack after school had let out, he noticed the substitute having a long, excited-looking conversation on the pay phone by the school playground.

That's strange, Diego thought. *Why wasn't Mr. Chaney using one of the regular phones inside the school?*

He slid his backpack down next to his bike and tiptoed cautiously over to the playground. Then he ducked behind the slide and poked his head out.

Mr. Chaney hadn't seen him.

Diego darted across the playground and into the kindergarteners' playhouse, which was right beside the pay phone. *Two can play this spy game,* he thought as he inched his way across the playhouse floor until he reached the window.

Now he could hear Mr. Chaney very clearly.

"They taste incredible!" he was saying. "They actually change flavors in your mouth!... No, I'm serious!"

Diego's heart began to pound. *I was right!* he said to himself. *He really is a spy!*

"Two kids came up with the idea," Mr. Chaney was saying. "But I've got a feeling one of them is the real brains behind it. Diego something, his name is. Seems he's kind of a genius. . . . No, he *claims* not to have a recipe," Mr. Chaney continued. "But I've got a feeling he's lying. . . . Yes, of course I'll keep working on him."

In the playhouse, Diego shivered.

Mr. Chaney laughed. It was not a pleasant sound.

"Hey, don't worry!" he said. "Have I ever let you down? I'll get that recipe by tomorrow afternoon. Then I'll report back to you. Okay, over and out!"

Chapter Seven

Spy Trapping

"Let's kill him!" Louie Watson bellowed.

"No, let's not go that far. Let's just sue him for everything he's got," Junior suggested.

"I don't think we should make him mad," Tiffany said fearfully. "What if he has some kind of laser gun or something and he tries to vaporize us? Why don't we just call the C.I.A.?"

"Come on, Tiffany," Bob said. "The C.I.A. will never believe a bunch of kids!"

"Yeah," Larry Watson agreed. "I think we should take care of this creep ourselves. Let's lock him in a locker and then break a bunch of rotten eggs over the vent holes."

"Yeah!" yelled Louie. "That's *better* than killing him! We'll *stink* him into making a confession!"

It was a half hour before school the next day, and the sixth-graders were hanging out on the jungle gym in the school playground—which Rocky insisted on calling "the scene of the crime."

Diego had phoned Bob and Rocky last night and told them about Mr. Chaney. The boys had decided to call the rest of the group for a meeting before school. But so far, no one could agree on just what to do about Mr. Chaney.

"Anyway, I'm not sure we should do anything," Chantilly said. "Doesn't it make more sense for Diego to tell Mr. Haypence about this, and let Mr. Haypence decide what to do?"

Scowling, Rocky shook his head. "We're the ones Mr. Chaney is out to get! We *deserve* to decide what to do with that sleazoid fake musician! And I think we should—"

"Hang on a minute, Rocky," Diego interrupted slowly. "I hate to say it, but Chantilly is right. We can't just go ahead and pulverize Mr. Chaney without telling Mr. Haypence.

"On the other hand," Diego went on, "Chantilly is also wrong. Mr. Haypence will just flap around when we tell him—he won't do anything useful. So let's have a plan ready for what we'll do *after* we tell him."

It turned out that Mr. Haypence didn't even flap around when Diego broke the news about Mr. Chaney. He just smiled in a dreamy kind of way.

"Good, good," he said, nodding. "I'm glad to see Mr. Chaney is taking an interest in our school's activities."

"Taking an interest!" Diego exploded. "He's taking *too much* interest, Mr. Haypence! Don't you think it's strange the way he—"

"I think it's even more peculiar to hear you questioning a teacher's judgment, Diego," Mr. Haypence broke in, in a sorrowful voice. *"Or* your principal's."

"But I—" Diego began. Mr. Haypence wouldn't let him finish.

"Believe me, I know what's best for Hollis Elementary School," he said. "And Mr. Chaney is what's best."

After that, Diego had no problem calling another meeting of his friends—a let's-get-revenge meeting.

"First of all," he told them, "I need to come up with a recipe to give Mr. Chaney."

"I don't get it!" said Rocky with a wounded look. "All of a sudden you're going to give him the recipe now? That seems—"

"I didn't say *the* recipe," said Diego with a grin. "I said *a* recipe. Listen, everyone, I think I've got a plan...."

"Hi, Mr. Chaney!" Diego called down the hall the next morning.

The substitute teacher was scuttling toward the music room with an armful of triangles. He turned around quickly at the sound of Diego's voice. Several of the triangles skidded out of his arms and dinged to the ground—except for the one that bonged onto Mr. Chaney's toe.

"Ouch!" said Mr. Chaney, struggling to keep the rest of the triangles from sliding away. "Oh, hello, Diego! How are the . . . the Planetary Popcorns, or whatever you call them?"

"They're doing great," Diego told him. "And I wanted to let you know that I found the recipe for them. I thought I had lost it, but here it is!"

And he held out an index card.

Mr. Chaney grabbed the card eagerly. That made him drop the rest of the triangles, but he ignored them. "Thanks! Thanks a lot!" he said. Then he looked more closely at the card, and his face fell. "Wow, this is a *long* recipe!" he said.

It certainly was. Diego had covered both sides of the card with tiny, tiny handwriting. And to make things even harder for Mr. Chaney, he had written as messily as he could.

"The recipe shouldn't be too hard to follow," he lied. "There are a lot of chemicals in it, but you can get them at any drugstore."

That part was true. Diego didn't want Mr.

Chaney to waste any time tracking down complicated ingredients.

"I'm sure I will! Thank you, Diego! I—I'll enjoy reading this when I'm not playing the piano, or whatever I do!"

And he raced off down the hall, clutching the index card tightly.

"He didn't even pick up the triangles," Diego told his friends at lunch. "One look at that card and he was out of there."

"I hope *someone* will pick them up," said Tiffany nervously. "Triangles on a floor could cause a lot of injuries, you know."

No one paid any attention to her. "What do we do now, Diego? " asked Bob.

Diego grinned. "Well, he's taken the bait. Now let's land him. Everyone meet at my locker after school, and we'll follow him home. I bet you anything that Mr. Chaney's going to try whipping up a few Space Crystals of his own—and we're going to be there when he does."

"Shh!" whispered Diego frantically. "Louie and Larry, can't you be quieter?"

"Hey, I'm walking as quietly as I can!" Larry blared as he stomped along. "It's not my fault Mr. Chaney's yard has such loud grass!"

Mr. Chaney's house was at the end of a deserted-looking block. That is, the block had looked deserted until five minutes ago, when Diego and his friends had begun walking down it. At the first house, Larry had tripped over the handle of a red wagon that was parked across the sidewalk. At the second house, Louie had barked his shin on a fire hydrant and let out such a holler that a baby started shrieking inside the house. After that Diego had made the twins walk in the street—until *both* of them banged into a parked car. Diego didn't think they had dented the car, but he was afraid to look too closely.

Now a small posse was sneaking up toward Mr. Chaney's house—if you could really call it sneaking when the Watson twins were along. Those who had volunteered for what Rocky called the "search and destroy" mission were Diego, Rocky, Bob, and Larry and Louie.

A few minutes ago they had seen Mr. Chaney dashing up the front walk, so they knew he was inside somewhere. But where?

"Let's try around back," Diego whispered. "Kitchens are usually in the back, and he's probably in the kitchen."

Everyone dropped to the ground and began crawling around the edge of the house.

"Hey! What are you guys doing?"

Diego froze, then slowly turned around. A dirty-faced little boy was staring at them through the fence that separated the house next door from Mr. Chaney's.

Diego scrambled on hands and knees toward him. "We're just playing a little game," he whispered, forcing himself to smile gaily. "Kind of like hide-and-seek. Okay?"

"Hey, I wanna play, too!" The little boy ran toward his house, yelling at the top of his lungs, "Mom! Hey, Mooooom! Mom?"

Diego crouched down in the long grass and held his head in his hands. Everyone else had flattened themselves against the lawn as soon as the kid had started shrieking. *Why me?* Diego thought gloomily. *If Mr. Chaney catches us out here, what will we tell him?*

The back door of the house next door banged open, and Diego could see the boy's mother standing there. "What is it, Tommy?"

"Mommy, these big kids said I could—"

"What is all that dirt on your face?" his mother cried, interrupting him. "Come in here right now and get washed! You look like you've been playing in a pigsty!"

"Awww, Mom!" Diego could hear Tommy's whining grow fainter and fainter as he disappeared into the house. *Whew!* he thought, thankful for fences and tall grass and dirt.

Diego gave a low whistle and started heading

toward the back of Mr. Chaney's house again. Rocky rustled up beside him.

"Boy, if we find Mr. Chaney's kitchen and he's in there eating a hero sandwich or something, I might lose it! I'm starving!" he whispered.

"There he is! There he is!" Diego hissed. "Everyone get down! And keep quiet! The window's open!"

The kitchen *was* around back, and Mr. Chaney *was* in it. His back was to the window—*thank goodness,* thought Diego—and with a large spoon in one hand he was stirring something on the stove.

In his other hand, Mr. Chaney held the recipe card Diego had given him. Diego and his friends could hear his voice drifting faintly through the open window.

"Add one tablespoon potassium carbonate and stir," he read aloud slowly. He stopped stirring and shook out a little mound of potassium carbonate from a tin on the counter. A cloud of white dust rose into the air, and Mr. Chaney started coughing. "This *can't* be right!" Diego heard him say between coughs. "No *way* is this stuff going to taste anything like those crystals!" But he bent his head toward the index card again.

"Hold your breath and get ready!" Diego

whispered to his friends. He knew what came after the potassium carbonate—and what was about to happen.

Quickly, each boy pulled a piece of cloth out of his pocket and tied it around the lower part of his face. It wasn't as good as a gas mask, but it would help a little. They'd all be better off than Mr. Chaney, anyway.

"Okay. One-half cup sulphur," Mr. Chaney muttered. He picked up a blue bottle and poured something into the saucepan on the stove.

Instantly the rottenest smell in the history of the world filled the kitchen and drifted out into Mr. Chaney's backyard. It was like a million rotten eggs, and probably strong enough to peel paint.

Diego smiled into the crook of his arm. His recipe had worked.

In the kitchen, Mr. Chaney dropped his spoon, grabbed a dishcloth, and pressed it to his face. He yanked the saucepan off the stove and threw it into the sink. Then he dashed out the back door and came staggering into his backyard.

"GET HIM!" yelled Diego.

And, with a flying tackle, Diego brought Mr. Chaney to the ground.

"What's going on here? Wait a minute!" protested Mr. Chaney.

But no one was in the mood to wait for anything.

It was pretty easy to overpower Mr. Chaney. After all, five against one is not exactly a fair fight. Before Mr. Chaney could move, he was surrounded on all sides.

"Now we've got you, you spy!" panted Rocky as he pinned Mr. Chaney's hands behind his back. "You'll be sorry you ever tried to steal ideas from *us!*"

"What are you talking about? I'm not a spy!" protested Mr. Chaney.

"Then who were you talking to on the phone yesterday?" Diego challenged him. "And why did you want our recipe so badly?"

Mr. Chaney took a deep breath. "Because I'm with NASA," he said. "I'm working undercover."

Everyone paused.

"Right!" said Rocky. "And I'm Superman!"

"It's true!" Mr. Chaney protested.

"Prove it!"

"Let me up, and I'll show you my identification!"

The guys all looked at each other. Bob raised his eyebrows questioningly. Rocky sighed. Diego shrugged. The Watsons had gotten tangled up with each other when they all tackled

Mr. Chaney. They were still wrestling with each other.

"Okay," Diego said finally, "let's see it."

"But don't try anything funny," Rocky warned him.

Slowly, Mr. Chaney reached into his pocket, flipped open his wallet, and handed it to Diego.

"'Delbert Chaney,'" Diego read aloud. "'Security director in charge of special projects.' He's telling the truth, guys. He isn't a spy after all."

There was another pause.

"I don't get it!" said Rocky. "If you're not a spy, then why are you always sneaking around?"

Mr. Chaney smiled wryly. "I was supposed to be *protecting* you from spies. NASA sent me out to keep an eye on the school while this was all going on. I kept trying to find out more about your project so that I could figure out the best way to keep it under wraps. It never occurred to me that you might think *I* was a spy, too."

"So you're not really a music teacher?" asked Bob.

Mr. Chaney grinned. "I don't see how anyone could think *that*. No, I don't know anything about music. We just thought that posing as a substitute teacher would be the best cover for me."

"But...but why did you want the recipe, then?" asked Diego.

"I only wanted to test it to make sure it would really work. As I'm sure you can imagine, NASA doesn't want you—or us—to be embarrassed on national TV."

Mr. Chaney turned to Diego. "I assume that *wasn't* the real recipe you gave me?"

"Right," said Diego sheepishly. "I just came up with something that I knew would stink you out of your kitchen so we could nab you. The real recipe is at home. You can try it if you want."

"Well, *we* all suspected you weren't a real music teacher," said Bob. "But docs Mr. Haypence know about it?"

Mr. Chaney chuckled. "He sure does. When NASA called him about planting me in your school as a substitute teacher, he agreed right away. I think he's pulled it off pretty well, don't you?"

"Pretty well? Unbelievably well!" said Diego in amazement. "I never realized he was such a good actor!"

He turned to Mr. Chaney. "I'm really sorry,"

he said. "I guess we jumped to conclusions. Me most of all."

"That's okay," said Mr. Chaney. "I would have suspected me, too, if I had been you."

"You don't have to leave now that we've blown your cover, do you?" asked Tiffany anxiously the next day when the rest of the sixth grade had learned the truth. "Because I think it would be nice to have you stick around, just in case any spies *do* try to steal our recipe."

"You've got me until the *Orion* takes off," promised Mr. Chaney. "I'd be grateful if you wouldn't tell the other grades about this, though. I'm having enough trouble controlling them as it is."

Chapter Eight

Uh-Oh!

"There," said Diego as he fastened down the last piece of packing tape. "The Space Crystals are on their way!"

He handed the box to the delivery man.

Diego and Rocky stood watching as the man carefully put the box holding the Space Crystals into the back of his truck. Then, with a wave, he backed out of the school parking lot and drove away.

"NASA, here they come!" sang Rocky. "And tomorrow, they'll be exploding all over the space station."

Tomorrow the *Orion* was taking off. Diego and Rocky had finished making the last batch of Space Crystals the day before. They had rushed them into the lunchroom this morning, all ready to go.

Unfortunately, they had forgotten to bring anything to put them in.

They had carried the Space Crystals to school in a plastic bag that had originally been used for oatmeal bread. Diego had taken it from his mother's plastic-bag collection under the kitchen sink. Somehow he had the feeling that it wouldn't look very impressive to the people at NASA.

"What will we do?" he groaned. "They'll just laugh when they see an old bag full of white stuff!"

"Don't worry about it! Use the lunchroom saltshakers!" Ms. Weinstock told him. "I think we can sacrifice them for the cause."

"Thanks, Ms. Weinstock," said Rocky. "That would be great." He raised his voice to a bellow. "HEY, EVERYONE! Get into the kitchen! We need to set up an assembly line!"

So while Louie and Larry Watson dumped the salt out of the lunchroom saltshakers, Jonathan and Tiffany carefully refilled them with Space Crystals. Meanwhile, Diego got a box ready, and Rocky telephoned the airport to tell the chartered-plane people the crystals would be ready to go in an hour.

And now the shakers were on their way—all except for the one saltshaker that was going to go into the Hollis trophy case as a permanent reminder of the space-food project.

Diego heaved a sigh of relief. "Now we can relax," he said. "When does everyone get here?"

"Soon," Rocky answered.

In a few minutes, Mr. Frantz would be arriving for the ceremonial placing of the saltshaker into the trophy case. With him would be newspaper and TV reporters from all over the city, as well as most of the sixth-grade parents. Diego figured that half of those parents would be carrying video cameras. With so much media attention on the way, he wished his hair weren't totally standing up on one side. He had slept on it wrong.

At least the lunchroom looked okay. Tiffany, Jennifer, and Chantilly had seen to that. Tiffany was working on one of her famous posters. (Tiffany made posters at the drop of a hat. She had made book-report posters, "Wipe Your Feet on the Mat" posters for rainy days, and even posters to decorate the inside of her locker.) This one said,

WELCOME TO HOLLIS, MR. FRANTZ!
WELCOME, REPORTERS AND PARENTS!
WELCOME TO THE SPACE-CRYSTAL
EXTRAVAGANZA!

WE DON'T HAVE ANY FREE SAMPLES,
THOUGH!

"What do you think?" she asked when she saw Diego looking over her shoulder.

"Looks good!" said Diego. "But did you really have to put in the free samples part?"

"But I thought that there might be a stampede if I didn't put it in! All those reporters might just *trample us into the ground* trying to get samples! It would be awful!"

Diego hid a smile. "I didn't think of that," he said gravely. "Well, then, Tiff, the poster is fine."

Chantilly was busily taping photographs of the *Orion* to the lunchroom walls. "I've been cutting them out of magazines for the past couple of weeks," she told Diego. "I thought they might come in handy sometime."

"Great," said Diego. Lowering his voice, he added, "They make a lot more sense than those tissue-paper roses Jennifer is putting on the doors. Why did she decide to do *that*?"

"Don't ask me," said Chantilly with a grin. "I said they didn't seem very space-y, but Jennifer said that there weren't enough flowers in space. That's why space stations are so unromantic, she said."

"Not enough flowers in space," Diego repeated thoughtfully as he strolled away. "Flowers can't grow where there isn't any atmosphere, you know. I wonder if—"

"THEY'RE HERE! THEY'RE HERE!" And Mr. Haypence tore into the lunchroom. "I just saw Mr. Frantz's limousine pull up," he gabbled. "And there are about twenty TV trucks behind *that*! I-I didn't prepare any kind of opening ceremony! What are we going to do?"

He was literally yanking at his hair, he was so upset.

"I want everyone outside right now," he said. "Let's line up in front of the school to welcome Mr. Frantz. A little greeting ceremony will look great on TV! Come on, people! Let's get *out* there!"

Mr. Haypence's frantic mood was contagious. Everyone lined up and began marching rapidly out the door.

When they were all outside, Mr. Haypence shouted, "Now, arrange yourselves!"

"What do you mean?" asked Jennifer. "I'm *already* arranged, thank you!"

"No, I mean arrange yourselves into some kind of nice little group! A . . . a formation!"

Sighing to themselves, the sixth-graders shuffled around a little bit until they had formed a big semicircle.

"Now, what should we sing?" asked Mr. Haypence.

"*Sing?*" repeated Rocky incredulously.

"Of course! A nice song of welcome would look just charming on television, don't you think?"

"There's not really time for that, Mr. Haypence," put in Ms. Weinstock. "*Next* time we can rehearse something."

Mr. Haypence looked disappointed, but there really *wasn't* any time now. A chauffeur was opening the back door of Mr. Frantz's limousine.

As Mr. Frantz came sweeping out of his car, Mr. Haypence rushed up to him. "Welcome, Harlan!" he called, trying not to look at the TV cameras. For a second Diego thought he was actually going to bow, but he didn't. "It's *so* nice to see you," he said. "Welcome to Hollis—and to our *Orion* space-food project!"

"*Orion* space-food project?" Diego muttered to Bob. "I didn't know it was called that! Mr. Haypence is pretty quick on his feet!"

Mr. Frantz gave Mr. Haypence a hearty handshake and then spread his hands wide. "Well, where is it?" he cried. "I can't wait to see it!"

Mr. Haypence chuckled indulgently. "Isn't it just like a great thinker to get right to the point like that! The space food is in the lunchroom, Harlan. And I think you'll be *very* impressed with it."

Then he herded everyone back into the lunchroom—Mr. Frantz, the TV and newspaper reporters, parents, and all the sixth-graders. There he proudly showed them the saltshaker full of Space Crystals.

"But that's just salt!" objected one reporter.

"I know that's what it appears to be," said Mr. Haypence mysteriously. "But in reality, it is something quite different." Then he herded everyone out of the lunchroom and down to the trophy case.

When everyone was gathered in front of the trophies, Mr. Haypence handed the saltshaker to Diego with a flourish. "Would you and Rocky please place this alongside Hollis's many, many other fine awards?" he asked.

Actually, there weren't that many. Hollis's athletes had never been the greatest. And the awards that *were* there were so weird that a saltshaker didn't look too out of place next to them. Still, Diego couldn't help feeling ridiculous as he and Rocky reached out to place the saltshaker next to the microphone-shaped trophy the Hollis Debate Club had won eighteen years before.

"Wait a minute!" said Mr. Frantz. "I want to *see* this salt!"

"It's not salt, Harlan," Mr. Haypence explained again.

"I don't care what it isn't! I want to see what it *is*! Let me try some!"

"Of... of course!" answered Mr. Haypence. He frowned at Diego and Rocky. "Hand over that saltshaker!" he ordered them.

Diego handed Mr. Frantz the saltshaker. Everyone watched, in breathless silence, while Mr. Frantz shook a few tiny white Space Crystals into his hand.

He stared at them, frowning slightly. "What does it do?" he asked.

"Just... just wait a minute," said Mr. Haypence. "You're in for the surprise of your life, I assure you!"

But nothing happened.

"What's going on?" Diego whispered to Rocky. "The crystals should be activating by now!"

"I don't know!" Rocky whispered back. "Maybe his hand's not hot enough or something!"

Certainly nothing at all was happening to the crystals.

Mr. Frantz lifted his hand and shook the crystals into his mouth. Then he lowered his hand again and stared at Mr. Haypence.

"It *is* salt," he said.

Chapter Nine

Salt in Space?

"No, it's not," said Mr. Haypence blankly.

Mr. Frantz turned to stare at him. "I *know* what salt tastes like, thank you! Try some yourself!"

"Of course I will!" And Mr. Haypence shook a few white crystals into his hand. "Maybe you were too impatient," he told Mr. Frantz kindly. "It takes a few seconds before—"

Mr. Haypence broke off and stared at the crystals in his palm. They weren't doing anything more there than they had been in Mr. Frantz's hand. "Hmmm," he said thoughtfully. "I see what you mean."

With a suspicious glance at Diego, he tossed the crystals into his mouth.

Mr. Haypence turned and glared at Diego. "Harlan is right!" he said angrily. "This *is* salt!

Your Space Crystals are plain old *salt!* What's going on here?"

"Young man," Mr. Frantz said to Diego, "I don't know what kind of trick you're trying to play, but I don't think it's very funny."

This can't be happening! Diego wanted to scream.

His mind was racing. Was it possible the Space Crystals lost their power after a couple of days? Or could there have been some salt left in the saltshakers he and Rocky had borrowed from Ms. Weinstock?

"I . . . I . . . I can't imagine what's going on," he stammered.

"I can!" chirped Larry Watson cheerfully. "I think it might have something to do with me and Louie! Kind of."

Everyone turned to stare at him.

"See, Louie and I were supposed to be emptying all the salt out of the saltshakers," Larry explained. "Only we were talking about this soccer game we saw on TV last night. So we probably forgot to empty out every single saltshaker. It's easy to forget what you're doing when you're talking about something, you know?"

"Larry, do you know what you're saying?" asked Diego. "We have no way of knowing whether we sent NASA plain old salt or Space Crystals!"

Larry just shrugged. "Hey, sorry!" he said. "Everyone makes mistakes, you know!"

"And this certainly is a mistake," muttered Mr. Frantz.

Tiffany burst into loud, sputtery tears. "What are we going to do?" she wailed. "We'll probably be arrested by NASA for tampering with government property!"

"And I'm going to be the laughingstock of the entire scientific community," added Mr. Frantz bitterly. "I wanted to give NASA something fun. *This* is not fun."

NASA...

"Hey, wait a minute!" said Diego suddenly. "Mr. Chaney can help!"

"What do you mean?" asked Ms. Weinstock. "Why should a music teacher be able to—"

But Mr. Haypence interrupted her. "*Excellent* suggestion, Diego!"

Diego was already out the door.

He raced down the hall, skidded around the corner, and burst into the music room without knocking.

"Mr. Chaney! Mr. Chaney! You've got to help us!" he shouted. "Thewrongsaltshakerswent-toNASAand—" He took a deep breath and started over. "The wrong saltshakers went to NASA by mistake," he gasped. "We sent them real salt, not Space Crystals. Can you help us?"

"And now we'd like to welcome you to A.M. *Pasadena*," said the announcer, "with your host, Mike McIntyre."

"Hi, Mike!" said Diego happily.

"I never thought I'd see a son of mine actually *talking to* the mind rotter," muttered Diego's father.

"Dad, shut up!" said Diego and Carlos in unison.

School was about to start, but this time no one in the Lopez family was worried about Diego's getting there on time. They were all too busy watching TV. The *Orion* would be taking off in a couple of hours, and for once, Diego's parents had suspended the anti-TV rules.

Mike McIntyre's grin filled the screen again. "Good morning, everyone," he said. "As most of our viewers in Pasadena probably know by now, the *Orion* space station takes off this morning. It's leaving earth a day late, for reasons NASA would not divulge."

"Thank you, NASA," said Diego fervently. "I'd hate it if everyone in the country knew we had been a day late getting the right crystals to mission control."

"But late or not," continued Mike McIntyre, "the *Orion* is going to be carrying a little bit of Pasadena with it."

"Awesome," said Diego.

"Kowabunga," agreed Rocky. He had biked over to watch the news with Diego before school.

"Under the direction of their principal, Mr. Wilfred Haypence, the sixth-graders at Pasadena's own Hollis Elementary School created a new space food for the *Orion's* crew," Mike McIntyre went on.

Now a picture of all the sixth-graders appeared on the screen. They were standing in front of the school and blinking into the sun.

Diego and Rocky were standing in front of the group, holding a saltshaker and staring sternly at the camera. They had *had* to look stern. Both of them were afraid they were going to crack up.

"Hey, there's D!" shrieked Carlos. "You're on TV, D! You're on TV! You're on—"

"I *know* I am," said Diego. He was staring at his TV self in dismay. "Look at the way my hair is standing up! Do I really look that stupid in real life?"

"Oh, yes," Rocky said confidently. "So do I. Don't worry about it."

"Ordinary salt, you say? Well, the answer is no," came Mike McIntyre's voice. "That salt-shaker is holding something called Space Crystals. According to Mr. Haypence, the crystals are the creation of two of Hollis's brightest sixth-graders—Diego Lopez and Rocky Latizano."

"*Bright!*" shouted Rocky. He punched Diego ecstatically on the shoulder. "Did you hear that? He said I was *bright*! Usually people just say I eat too much!"

"Mr. Haypence added that none of the sixth-graders' efforts would have amounted to anything without Hollis Elementary School's state-of-the-art lunchroom," continued Mike McIntyre. "He invited our camera crew to photograph the lunchroom, but we were unfortunately out of time."

"Haypence must have been heartbroken," said Diego with a grin. "The one chance he had to get the lunchroom on TV, and it didn't happen!"

"Well, congratulations to all the sixth-graders at Hollis," said Mike McIntyre. "We understand that Space Crystals are so spectacular that NASA is actually considering marketing them commercially. Who knows? Perhaps Space Crystals may someday take their place alongside Milky Ways, Starbursts, and Mars bars in the great galaxy of candy brands.

"And now we have startling news about some chimps at the Pasadena Playhouse," Mike McIntyre went on, before Mr. Lopez vaulted out of his seat and turned off the set.

"That's enough mind rotting for now," he said. "But congratulations, Diego. We're really proud of you."

Diego's mother walked over to Diego and gave him a big hug. "Congratulations, honey," she said. "And to you, too, Rocky."

"I didn't know NASA might actually start selling Space Crystals!" said Diego. "That's fantastic! I wonder if our pictures will be on the wrappers?"

Rocky smiled at him. "I hope so. As long as they don't use the picture they just showed on TV."

"Diego, is something happening to your cheeseburger?" Rocky asked a few hours later. "Because if something's *not* happening to mine, then I'm going crazy."

The *Orion* had taken off safely, and now it was time for the Hollis sixth-graders to try to return to normal life. The camera crews were gone. So was Mr. Chaney. He had gone back to NASA, and in his place was a new substitute music teacher. She really seemed to know about music. You could tell from the fact that she sang the roll call every day.

Mrs. Doubleday's class had spent the morning relearning about decimal points, India, and punctuation, as well as the other subjects they'd been working on before the space-food project came along. It was hard work getting back into the swing of regular classes. By the time lunch rolled around, everyone was ready for it.

Luckily lunch was cheeseburgers and french fries—a meal you didn't have to work hard to like. Unluckily, something seemed to be *happening* to the cheeseburgers and french fries. And it wasn't just Rocky's imagination.

Diego stared down at his plate. "This isn't possible," he breathed.

His cheeseburger was pulsing with a strange, unearthly purple light. The cheese seemed to be melting—or was it changing into something else? And his french fries were starting to move gently around his plate, all by themselves.

"It's possessed!" moaned Tiffany.

"I don't think that's it," said Rocky grimly. "Diego, are you thinking what I'm thinking?"

"I don't see what else it could be," Diego answered. "Let's go check."

The two boys stood up and walked slowly into the kitchen. "Ms. Weinstock," Diego asked, "where are the saltshakers?"

"Right over there," Ms. Weinstock told him, pointing at a countertop.

Diego picked one of them up and shook a few grains into his hand. He hardly needed to. He knew what was going to happen—and it did. In a few seconds, the white grains exploded into a handful of brightly colored Space Crystals.

Diego turned to Rocky with a wan smile. "I guess we mixed the saltshakers up again when we were repacking the box for NASA," he said. "We must have sent some Space Crystals and some salt, just like before. And whoever opened the box at NASA must have tried a saltshaker with real Space Crystals in it, so they didn't realize anything was wrong."

"Guess so," said Rocky in a sickly voice. "And I guess that Space Crystals act even *weirder* when you put them on food instead of in your hand. And I guess that some of the astronauts will get real Space Crystals, and some of them will get dud Space Crystals."

"And some of them will have ordinary salt on

their food, and some of them will have *weird* salt on their food," said Diego. "The question is, who will get what? And what will happen when they find out?"

But there was no one to answer these questions. The *Orion* was already speeding away into outer space.